# Sugar Time

# Other Books by Joy V. Smith

## Detour Trail

## The Doorway and Other Stories

## Hidebound

## Strike Three

The first three *Sugar Time* stories are also available as an audio book from Hadrosaur Productions. www.hadrosaur.com

# Sugar Time
# Joy V. Smith

Hadrosaur Productions, Mesilla Park, NM

Sugar Time
Hadrosaur Productions
First Edition, first printing, continuous printing on demand
First date of print publication: August 2015
Author: Joy V. Smith, www.pagadan.wordpress.com
Editor:  David Lee Summers, www.davidleesummers.com
Cover Art: Laura Givens, www.lauragivens-artist.com

ISBN: 1-885093-81-0

Hadrosaur Productions
P.O. Box 2194
Mesilla Park, NM 88047-2194
www.hadrosaur.com

This is a work of fiction.  Names, characters, places, and incidents are
products of the author's imagination or are used fictitiously.

# Table of Contents

To all my editors, including David Lee Summers who edited this work, for their support!

# Sugar Time

# Sugar Time

She was standing on the porch, staring doubtfully at the oddly featureless door of the ornate blue, gray, and lilac Victorian when the two men came up the walk behind her. Though they were both big men, they moved lightly up the porch steps. The one with the red hair was a couple inches shorter and a little heavier than his companion. They weren't Samuels and Bartow, and the sudden flicker of relief died. Then she took a second look at the redhead.

He spoke first. "Do you live here, Miss?" he asked in a cool, official tone. "We got a report of funny noises coming from here." He paused. "Like screams."

*Oh great,* she thought, *funny noises, screams, and him. Just what I need.* She took the badge and looked expectantly at the other man; he looked at her appraisingly as he handed her his badge. The men towered almost a foot above her slight figure as she studied the badges carefully, brown eyes intent. The redhead was Izaak Walton and her cousin; the blackhaired one was Francisco Reyes. She considered. They might be useful. On the other hand, could she risk it? Still, she didn't have much choice.

"Aunt Cecilia said you'd been promoted to homicide, Izzy," she said finally. "Congratulations. How come you're here?"

The redhead smiled, reaching for his badge. "Cousin Sunny got the call. It's Grandfather's old house, and I knew Uncle Max hadn't sold it yet, so I thought I'd check it out. Frank, meet my little and youngest cousin." He stopped. She'd moved next to him and was balancing slightly on one foot. Small and dainty but quick, he remembered. He said, "Can you get us into the house?"

"Yes," she said, relaxing a little, "that's why I'm here my-self—to look around. Uncle Max couldn't reach anyone here and sent me over."

"Why you?" asked Frank curiously.

"He trusts me," she replied, standing a little straighter. "And so does Japheth," she added, looking towards a young black man, who had just rounded the corner of the house.

"Nothing to see. Tight as a drum," he reported, looking inquiringly at the two men on the porch.

"Police," she told him. "They're coming in with us and help us look around." She introduced them. "This is Japheth Johnson, my associate. Japheth, meet Izaak Walton and Frank Reyes. Izaak also happens to be my cousin." She looked earnestly at them and said again, "Japheth knows me and trusts me." She ignored his quick, sideways glance.

"Now I'm telling all of you—Let me go first. Stay behind me. If you see something odd that needs investigating, bring it to my attention; don't be macho and barge in front of me." She looked straight at Izzy. "Otherwise I will just heave your bodies out the nearest window whenever I get around to it."

All three looked at her curiously. She hoped they were giving her the benefit of the doubt, but she did have to warn them. Also, she was quite adept at avoiding introducing herself. She'd managed to stop Izzy, for the moment anyway.

She turned her attention back to the door and scanned it deliberately, concentrating on the bottom part of the door, and saw nothing. Sighing, she dropped to her knees and asked the men who crowded round her, also staring at the door, "Does anyone see anything that looks like a slot down here?" Now they all were crouching around her.

Japheth reached out to run his hand over the wood. "Maybe…" He started as she grabbed his hand hastily.

"Don't touch anything!" She caught her breath. "Get back. Wait." She pulled a flat, folded piece of metal out of her pants pocket. "Drat," she muttered, as she crouched on the ground staring at the door and trying to remember what she had been told about the slot's location. It was towards the bottom, he'd said. As she shifted her position, the key passed in front of the door, and a piece of wood slid sideways, revealing the slot.

"Wow, magnetic," murmured Japheth appreciatively.

She stood up, resisted the urge to dust herself off, and slid the key into the slot, which was, naturally enough, not at ground level. As the door opened, she stepped inside and turned to face the three men.

She spoke slowly, seriously, "Walk behind me single file. Do not touch anything. The things inside this first room are designed to attract people. If one of you feels he must touch something, please wait till the rest of us are out of the room so we are not hit by flying debris. Do you understand what I am saying?" As one, they nodded and waited patiently for her to lead the way. Izzy was as quiet and puzzled as the other two. She wished she didn't have the feeling that they were humoring her.

The room was dimly lit, but some things seemed to stand out ... glittering, scattered shapes on a table ... a gleaming exotic form on the bookcase ... pictures on the wall that appeared to show...

*Good Lord*, she thought, *I never realized...*

"Wow," muttered Japheth, "I never realized..."

She almost turned to ask him what, but caught herself in time. Izzy muttered something too low to catch. Frank hissed softly once, but was otherwise silent. They finally exited the room and paused just outside.

"What next?" Frank was the first to ask. No one mentioned the room and its contents.

"Just be careful," she said slowly. "Tell me if you see anything suspicious. Don't touch anything or shoot anything without asking me first."

"Like what?" asked Frank, with a hint of impatience.

"What if there's no time?" added Izzy, with forced reasonableness.

"What about cats, Sugar?" Japheth was staring suspiciously at a huge, striped gray cat that was staring suspiciously back. Then he noticed Frank's speculative look. Izzy only smiled to himself. "That's her name, dammit. I swear to God that's her name," he said defensively.

"My name is Sugar. Sugar Sweet," she affirmed sharply. "Just never, ever call me Sweetie."

Izzy shrugged, a smug expression on his face. "People in glass houses..."

Frank was a little dazed. *That explains the cinnamoncolored hair and eyes like chocolate fudge,* he thought.

And then they all looked at the cat; it slowly bottled its tail and began to arch its back.

Sugar backed away. "It's a watch cat. Just leave it alone and don't do anything suspicious."

"A watch cat. Of course. I should have known," said Izzy.

"Why?" said Japheth, a little resentfully. "I wouldn't have known."

Sugar stood near the door leading to the next room and looked at them. She was grateful not only not to be alone here, but to have these three with her. She hoped she could trust them. She gave a last puzzled look at the cat.

"Let's go," she told them, leading the way into the next room. This room, like the others, was obviously part of a very old house. Its fireplace was apparently tile, though it was hard to tell under the dust and dirt.

"Not very tidy, are they?" remarked Japheth casually.

"You've never been here before, have you?" said Frank thoughtfully. "Has she?"

Japheth shrugged. Frank looked at Sugar, who was thinking deeply. Worried? Frank wondered, moving a little towards her before thinking better of it.

Izzy caught her attention. "Sugar. That cat's following us."

"Of course," she told him shortly. "It's a watch cat."

"Of course," he retorted. "I forgot." He couldn't make a dramatic exit, because it might not be safe. They couldn't help noticing that Sugar kept a wary eye on the cat also.

She led the way to the next room. Going through a short, dark hall and then a pantry, they entered the kitchen. Sugar opened the refrigerator and stared into it briefly before shutting it firmly and turning away. She sighed.

Frank glanced at her and then the fridge and went to open it himself, giving her plenty of time to stop him. "So," he said, speaking to them all, "no one's been here for some time."

Izzy shook his head, puzzled. "There's water in the cat's dish," he pointed out, "and it must be eating or, knowing cats, it would be in here, asking for food. Even if it is a watch cat."

"Mice?" questioned Frank. "It's an old house."

Japheth spoke then, a little sharply. "Anyone notice there's an awful lot of dishes here for one cat."

"There is more than one cat," Sugar told them. "Samuels and Bartow, who are supposed to be in charge here, have collected some exotic animals in their travels." She'd decided it was about time to give them a few hints. The next room she took them into was large, dimly lit and obviously used for storage.

"Look, Sugar," said Izzy casually, "there are two more cats in the window."

They all looked. Looking back were two cats, but not cats; they were large, taking up most of the double window seat they sat on. They seemed to be a dull yellow as far as could be seen in the light filtering through the dirty window. Their fur was coarse and stiff, sticking straight out from their bodies; it was thicker, longer, and darker around the neck. Their heads were awfully pointed and narrow—for cats. They didn't appear to have tails. Then one closed its round yellow eyes, which disappeared, completely covered by the coarse hair.

"Neat trick," remarked Izzy, not as casually as he had intended this time.

"Talk to me, Sugar," Frank told her. "Tell us about these two."

"Sugar, the watch cat won't come into this room." Japheth wanted her attention too.

"This isn't its territory, Japheth." She hoped that was the reason. "Frank, it's all right. These must be the Chessies my uncle told me about. I must talk to these two." She ignored the curious looks the three men gave her.

Her uncle had told her about them of course, and she wondered how she could have mistaken what was probably an ordinary cat for one of them. She hadn't realized they would look so alien.

She approached them slowly, stopping at a nonthreatening distance. They watched her intently. She figured they had to be as wary as she was. "I was sent here by my Uncle Maxwell Sweet," she explained. "He wants me to check into the project."

They all listened with interest.

She waited for a response, but turned away finally, trusting that they had understood her, or, failing that, in her companions' protection. Going on to the next door, which was closed, she stood in front of it. She wondered if she would have gone on if she were alone. She felt confident enough now; though, as the men crowded around her again, she hoped someone was watching the two Chessies.

This door, like the first, outside door, was devoid of openings or hardware. She pulled out the flat key and passed it over the door; once again a slot appeared, into which she inserted the key. Japheth watched with interest; the mechanism still fascinated him. Izzy was keeping a watchful eye on their new companions, which now flanked the little group. So it was Frank who pointed out an interesting fact about the room they were about to enter.

"This looks like an addition. What about this wall, Sugar?" She had paused before opening the door; now she turned, not averse to postponing it a little longer.

"This part of the building is an addition; it's reinforced concrete and steel. There are two rooms in the addition." She glanced at the Chessies before turning back to the door.

Pausing just inside a brightly lit room which apparently ran the width of the house, she announced, after a quick look around, "the laboratory." It was a laboratory, and it contained three desks with computers, assorted machines, storage cabinets, cages, and two long stainless steel tables. She'd expected something like that and looked resignedly at the double doors with the metallic sheen on the other side of the room.

"Damned impressive." Japheth was admiring the computers and other equipment which filled the room. "State of the art."

"Look, but don't touch," Sugar told him. "Not yet."

He moved away from the computer he was studying and looked her in the eyes. "So this is why I'm here," he said softly.

"Yes. It's yours if you want it," she said with sudden decision, "but it's important; it's secret; it could be dangerous. You've a lot to learn about the project. You were recommended because you're not only good with computers and other machines." She stopped and looked meaningfully at him before continuing. "But you have integrity. Both are important here."

She left him to think about it. She walked slowly among the machines; they didn't tell her anything, and she ended up beside Frank. Izzy was roaming the lab looking thoughtful.

"Francisco," she said. "Do you really prefer Frank? I like Francisco. Of course, if I were screaming for help, I would probably use Frank." He considered her for several moments before he relaxed into a smile and admitted, "Some call me Francisco. You are welcome to do so if you wish." He became serious again as he asked, "Tell me why you might be screaming for help."

Izzy joined Japheth, and they watched the two Chessies lying Sphinxlike in front of the double doors, facing them and waiting. Japheth, pondering his decision, idly asked, "So your mother liked Biblical names too, huh?"

"Yeah, and my father liked fishing so they compromised." Izzy shrugged.

Japheth was a little puzzled. "What do you mean?"

"If you don't know, I sure ain't going to tell you," Izzy said, relieved, and looked towards Sugar and Frank. "I don't think we're done here yet," he added.

"No," Japheth agreed, and they went to join the other two.

Sugar had waited before answering Frank; now she spoke to them all. "I don't know what's behind these doors. There's a good chance that there is nothing there. There probably *is* nothing there. But I can't be sure about that."

"Izzy and I better take over then. We've gone through lots of doors. You and Japheth stay clear." Frank had his gun out and was already turning toward the doors, when Sugar stepped in front of him, ending up between the Chessies which had turned their attention from the doors and were watching the humans curiously.

"It's not that simple." Sugar was torn between irritation and appreciation. "The doors open with a combination I have, unless it's been changed. Uncle Max has been ill and out of touch. And," she went quickly to a big cabinet, "here are some weapons that may be more useful." She opened one of the cabinet doors and lifted a big gun from its rack. It was one of an assortment of guns.

Izzy whistled in awe as he examined an even bigger gun. "Now that's a gun," he said. "What have you and Uncle Max been up to? I didn't think scientists went in for this sort of thing." He stared at Sugar in delighted surprise.

"Do you really think we're going to need one of these?" asked Frank quietly.

Japheth was studying the gun assortment too. "Maybe we should just nuke it," he suggested.

Sugar shook her head. "I want to know what's behind the doors. Besides, most of these are just for tranquilizing."

"Are you any good with this gun?" Frank demanded. When

she shook her head again, he reached for the gun. She hesitated briefly before giving it to him.

"I'd feel better with a gun too," she informed him a little stiffly.

"You concentrate on the doors," he told her, swinging around to cover them. "I'll be close, but not right next to you. We don't want one target. Izzy, you get farther to the left, and Japheth, if you can't help, stay out of the way."

"Yes, Japheth," Sugar added, "we may need someone to pick up the pieces." She turned her attention to the doors and to the Chessies.

"Perhaps one of you should be on each side." She didn't wait to see what they thought about it, but reached forward and ran through a color sequence on the multihued circle on the lefthand door.

The doors swung outward towards the little group, catching Sugar by surprise. As she stepped backward, she caught her first glimpse of what lay beyond. Feeling sick to her stomach delayed any response she might have made, but the creature inside dropped the arm he was gnawing and swung up his massive axe instantly.

Frank knocked her back to safety, throwing off his aim and inadvertently getting in Izzy's line of fire, but one Chessie seized the creature's leg as it charged them, while the other sprang on his chest. The creature was still amazingly quick; he pulled the snarling Chessie off his chest and bashed the other with his axe, sending them both flying. Frank stepped forward then and shot him in the head with his automatic.

Sugar had picked herself up and was fighting the feeling of nausea. Frank spoke sharply to Japheth, "Make yourself useful and find something to cover the bodies with."

Sugar intervened hastily. "No. I'll be all right. We have to find out what happened first. But we'll need something to wrap them in after we get them out of the machine, and they'll have to be disposed of somehow." She frowned and looked up to find Frank looking at her intently. She turned quickly to Izzy and asked, "What does it look like to you, Izzy."

"Not good," he retorted, "but we need more input."

Japheth looked defiantly at Frank and said, "I think I can

help. The Chessies and this caveman type aren't from around here, not from now anyway." He looked at Sugar. "Did you know that I was interested in time machines?" he asked.

"We knew you had an open mind on the subject and were well qualified in other respects also. I hope you'll join our project." She turned to Izzy and Frank. "This has to be kept secret. I hope you can see that. In fact, I would like you two to join us also." She looked at them hopefully. She wasn't sure what she'd do if they didn't agree to at least keep quiet about the project. Of course, Izzy had always been the adventurous sort. That was one reason he'd joined the police force.

Leaving the three of them to think about it, she went reluctantly towards the time machine and recalled immediately the two Chessies, observing with relief that they were both alive. The larger Chessie was cleaning thoroughly with its tongue the bloody gash in the other's shoulder. "I'm sorry. Are you all right? Do you need help? And I want to thank you for helping us." It was difficult talking to someone who apparently couldn't talk back. She wasn't even sure they understood her. She wondered if her uncle was right about them.

They both looked at her intently, and the smaller one put out one massive paw and touched her hand lightly. Then they turned their attention back to each other.

The three men watched and listened. Japheth spoke first. "She needs us. Hell, I need you anyway. I sure hope you'll help us clean up this mess."

Frank looked at him, "So you are going to join her project."

Izzy spoke musingly, "I'd hate to see them try to get along without us. I had no idea she and Uncle Max were having such fun." He glanced slyly at Frank. "You wouldn't let her go off in that machine by herself would you?"

Frank looked at Sugar and frowned. "Let's see what she wants us to do first," he suggested.

Later they all stood around the time machine. "It's obvious the cave man got into the machine with them, killed them, and then was trapped here with the bodies. You can hardly blame him for…" Izzy trailed off and shrugged.

Sugar nodded, lips shut tightly.

Japheth interjected quickly, after looking at her, "Where

did they come from? What are their scientific names? I've never heard of Chessies, and they sure don't look familiar."

Sugar glanced gratefully at him. "They haven't been identified from fossil records, according to Uncle Max, but that doesn't prove anything," she said pensively. "I think Chessie comes from Cheshire. We've seen why they called them that."

Japheth was caught up in the subject now. "How shall we classify them then?"

"I'll go through their record books," looking involuntarily at the time machine. "If they've already done that … It's the least we could do."

Izzy broke in. "Frank and I should be getting back. After we report that we checked everything out really thoroughly and found nothing of interest…" He looked questioningly at Frank, who nodded. Izzy continued, "we'll be back to discuss the future. It might be interesting to work with you. I always thought you'd made a mistake studying history. But maybe you had a plan, huh?"

Sugar smiled at him blandly. "I'm looking forward to having you on the project."

He looked at her sharply, but nodded.

Izzy paused just after going out the final door, "What about Uncle Max?" he asked Sugar. She had accompanied him and Frank to be sure they made it out safely.

"You know he's very ill," she said worriedly, suddenly reminded. She stepped outside, reaching out tentatively. "It's just us."

"Us is enough," said Izzy, touching her briefly on the shoulder.

"Yes," said Frank, looking at her quietly and resisting the urge to touch her. "We'll be back as soon as we can. Wait for us."

She smiled at him. "Of course," she said.

The Chessies had followed them down and were peering curiously out the door. In the darkness of the room, Mingus grinned at Rell. "Maybe landing here wasn't a mistake."

Rell looked at him resignedly. "Be more careful this time," she told him.

# Flight Test

Sugar stood in the doorway of the lab and surveyed the time machine. It had been cleaned up and the bodies disposed of, though that was only temporary. Now it was just her, Japheth, the Chessies, and a faint lingering odor of disinfectant. As she climbed into the machine and studied the control panel, Japheth watched her uneasily. "You promised Frank you'd wait," he said.

"Dolt. That'll make her do it for sure." Japheth looked in disbelief at the Chessies. The smaller one gazed at him calmly. The other glared at its companion, yellow eyes slitted, and one massive yellow paw raised as if in threat. It looked very catlike at the moment.

"Uhh, Sugar," Japheth said shakily, staring at the Chessies

She turned sideways on the seat and looked at them with interest. "What did I miss?" she asked.

"One of them spoke to me," he told her. "I think…" He ran a hand through his short, tightlycurled hair. "I think it was telepathy."

"Uncle Max suspected something like that," she said with satisfaction. "What did it say?"

Japheth looked at the Chessies uncertainly.

The small Chessie looked at Sugar. "I merely wondered if you shouldn't study their records first." Its companion grunted, and its eyes disappeared into its coarse hair. That, however, they had grown accustomed to.

"I wasn't going to go far," Sugar said, half seriously as she led the way back to the lab. She paused suddenly in the doorway. "What are you called?" She could learn that at least.

"I am Mingus," the small Chessie told her, "and my mate is Rell. And usually," he said slyly, "she is very talkative." The other Chessie sniffed and turned away.

Sugar saw that she had no intention of talking to them and went on into the lab, shutting the double doors behind her. "You're the computer expert, Japheth," she said. "You can look there for records; I'll check the desks."

It was just over an hour later that she straightened up from poring over the assorted notebooks and papers she'd found in the first two desks. "Nothing here but expense accounts, appointments, and data copied from books, history mostly. I recognize some of the references. There's a shopping list here too. Looks like they planned to buy a lot of cat food. How are you doing?"

Japheth scowled at the computer screen. "Nothing here. They've got these records locked up tight."

"Rell could help," Mingus informed them. "She was watching at least twice from the examining table while Samuels entered the data Bartow gave him."

Japheth swiveled to look at the tables on the other side of the lab. "Wow. You've got good eyes."

Rell padded over to Japheth's chair and stared unblinkingly at him until he surrendered it. She jumped onto the chair and began hitting the keyboard, stubby fingers whipping in and out of the coarse hair.

"Chessies have fingers," whispered Japheth to Sugar.

He had circled the chair, and they both watched the screen over Rell's back.

"*Tempus Fugit*," said Sugar.

Japheth groaned. "I never would have thought of that," he said.

"It's the name of the time machine," Mingus told them.

"I like it, "Sugar said.

They watched as Rell scrolled the last recorded report.

"To have survived so much," Sugar said regretfully.

"Dinosaurs," muttered Japheth. "I hope you don't have a yen for dinosaurs, Sugar."

"We'd need a bigger machine." She considered a moment, then laughed. "No, I don't think so. They're even scarier than I imagined." She stretched and looked at her watch. "It's getting late. Want to send out for a pizza?"

"Not tonight. I've got lots to do if you're planning any trips." He looked at her questioningly.

"Bring back some suggestions," she told him. "We'll discuss them in the morning."

"You really want my input?" he asked diffidently.

"That's why I'm hiring you, Mr. Johnson," she told him in

accentuated formal tones and raised her eyebrows.

He turned to go, then paused and came back. "What about returning an overdue library book?" he asked.

Sugar frowned as she considered it. "I don't think so," she said slowly. "The time is too close to now. If you were on campus, or even if you weren't, someone might notice."

He shrugged, disappointed. "I thought it was something we could check out with the time machine, so to speak."

She laughed. "I am looking forward to working with you, Japheth. Be here about ten. I'll be stopping by to see Uncle Max before I come."

After he left, Mingus sat down in front of her. "What's a pizza?" he asked patiently.

"You'll like it," she promised.

* * *

Next morning Japheth was waiting for her on the wide porch of the old Victorian. "Sorry I'm late," she told him. "Uncle Max was feeling better so we talked a while." She bent forward to insert the flat metal key into its slot. Her long brown hair fell forward and brushed the door. She pushed it back quickly. She was always careful when entering the house.

"I'm glad," he said. "I'd like to talk to him."

Sugar straightened and looked at him. "I hope it doesn't bother you to be working for a woman," she said stiffly.

"I hope you're not accusing me of prejudice, ma'am. You're more likely to have trouble with Frank what'shisname and your cousin," he said, a little resentfully.

"I'm sorry," she said. "It's not your fault I'm feeling inadequate this morning." After a thoughtful pause, she went on. "They're macho, but I don't expect to have any trouble working with Izzy or his partner—Francisco Reyes," she reminded him. "And we'd probably be dead if they hadn't been there when the Neanderthal jumped us."

"True enough," he said, remembering his introduction to the time machine and its grisly contents. "So, are you planning any time trips for today?"

Sugar sighed. "Uncle Max told me I had to learn to walk before taking the bit in my teeth and galloping off in all directions," she explained and opened the door. Japheth gave her plenty of room as they went in. They walked carefully through that first dimly lit room with its assorted fatal attractions.

Mingus, Rell, and the gray tabby were waiting for them in the kitchen. "Pizza for breakfast would be good," Mingus suggested. There was a hint of agreement from Rell. She'd really liked that pizza.

"I didn't pick anything up because I was running late," Sugar said in dismay. She looked towards the lab with regret. "You start work on the records, Japheth. I'll get some groceries." She paused and looked at him. "Do you cook?" she asked hopefully.

"Don't look at me," he told her. "That's not in my job description."

She was back in less than hour and maneuvered her way carefully, one bag at a time, through the first room. Rell joined her in the kitchen and watched with interest as she cleaned out the refrigerator before emptying the bags. "I bet cat food gone bad is one of the worst smells in the world," Sugar said aloud as she dumped it in the waste basket.

Rell pulled her head out of a bag, and Sugar managed not to giggle. "It didn't smell that good when it was fresh," she said. "We used to sneak out at night and raid the refrigerator. It made them suspicious, but it's a good thing we could open the cage locks, or we would have starved when they didn't come back."

Sugar dished out fresh food for Torquata sitting patiently at her feet and listened with avid interest. She wondered again how she could have ever mistaken the big gray housecat for a Chessie.

"They would have returned us like they did the rest of the fauna they collected," Rell continued, "but they couldn't understand the test results. We didn't want to go back; we decided to talk to your uncle, but he never returned."

"He worried about you," Sugar told her, "when he became ill and couldn't contact Samuels and Bartow. I was still in school, and he didn't trust anyone else." She turned to unpack the remaining bag. "How's Japheth doing?"

"We found the fuel dump, "Rell said complacently.

Sugar blinked, threw the rest of the food in the fridge, and made for the lab. "Tell me about the fuel," she demanded.

Japheth sat at the computer, brown fingers busy on the

keys. "And print ... the formula will be easier to work with this way," he explained.

She looked at the screen in fascination. "The formula for fuel," she breathed.

"No, the fuel is in the basement, as safe as concrete and stainless steel can make it, because it is basically toxic waste."

"Toxic—shit!" she said.

He smiled slightly. "Yes, that's another name for waste," he agreed. "Samuels obtained it somehow, but I haven't found out where. But there's a lot of it."

"What's the formula for then?"

"How much power is needed to get someplace? It takes more power to go somewhere than somewhen. Come on. I want to check the mechanism," he said, shoving his chair back.

Inside the huge room with its vaulted ceiling, they paused to admire the time machine. It was the size of a van and painted in shades of camouflage brown. Tinted windows wrapped all the way around it. A huge bumper covered the entire bottom of the vehicle. Inside, a bench seat faced the control panel that covered the entire front up to the windows. There was a space of about two feet between the seat and the solid barrier behind it, with a sliding door that led to the cargo area.

Japheth slipped behind the seat and inserted a key into the floor; a portion of which slid sideways. Sugar knelt on the seat, now covered by an old green spread, and looked over the back of the seat in fascination. Japheth cautiously reached down, pushed a hidden button, and a boxlike container arose. "What's that for?" she asked.

"Ease and safety of loading. And it stores four extra blocks so there's plenty of fuel." He gave the box a shove, and it quietly retracted. Japheth slid out of the machine. "It is a pleasure working with everything those two did," he said in sincere admiration.

"My uncle was responsible for some of this too," Sugar reminded him sharply.

"I know," he said smoothly. "It's in the records. That's why I'm looking forward to meeting him. But what about Frank and Izzy? Have you heard from them?"

"Tonight Uncle Max and tomorrow Frank and Izzy," she told him.

"If you two are finished," Rell said plaintively, "what about dinner?"

In the kitchen, Sugar watched Rell finish off a ham sandwich, learning to recognize contentment on that alien face. Mingus and Japheth had just agreed to split a cheese sandwich when a bonging began that reverberated through the whole house.

Japheth and Sugar looked at each other blankly. "Someone's coming," Mingus told them. "The alarm is triggered by any approach. The monitor is in the lab." He jumped down from the table and headed there.

What monitor?" Sugar asked plaintively.

Japheth shrugged. "When are you going to put them on the payroll?"

"They did help save our lives," she replied. "And they don't want to go back. Have you wondered any about that? Or where they came from originally?"

He shook his head decisively. "Tell me what you find out," was all he said. In the lab, monitor screens now covered the wall facing the desks. Each room showed up clearly, also the yard, porch, and sidewalk.

"It's Izzy." Sugar sounded disappointed

Rell and Mingus looked at each other. "He can tell you where Frank is," Rell reassured her.

"Why don't you bring him up, Sugar?" Japheth suggested.

"I prefer to spend as little time in the twilight zone as possible."

"No need to tell him about us yet," Rell cautioned.

"No," she agreed, thinking as she went to the door, about how easily she and Japheth had accepted the two Chessies. She really should learn where they came from…

She let Izzy in, but they didn't speak till they left that first room. "There's a problem," Izzy told her. "Frank and I thought we'd better stay on the force a while so you have someone on the inside. They're looking for Samuels and Bartow."

Sugar shivered, thinking of the three bodies in the freezer. When they reached the library, she stopped. "There's nothing better I'd like than to dispose of those bodies," she told him. "I've thought about using the time machine to dump them in a car or plane accident, but what about the marks on the bones?"

Izzy nodded. "A forensic pathologist would certainly wonder about that, which is why I'm here—to see how badly they've been chewed up."

Sugar swallowed. "I'll wait for you here," she told him. When he came back, she was sitting at the massive library table. She'd pushed aside the volumes that littered the table to make room for a map. Izzy pulled out a chair and sat next to her, gazing curiously at the Texas road map.

Sugar traced a route with her finger from Bryan to Galveston. "How about if they hired a boat and went out into the Gulf or even the ocean on some underwater archeological project?"

"What are a physicist and a zoologist doing on this project?" he asked caustically. "Anyway, Samuels missed two lectures and Bartow a week of classes. They weren't the kind to do that."

"Of course not," she said, glaring. "Obviously something happened to them. They used to go time tripping on weekends and vacations. Why not a fishing trip or something? We'd use the time machine to take them back." She paused. "Has it ever occurred to you how handy the time machine would be for alibis?"

Izzy grunted. The green eyes that usually looked on the world with amusement were serious. "Yeah," he said softly. "That's one reason Frank and I are joining you."

"Doing your civic duty?" she asked sharply.

You're my cousin," he said with a slow and tolerant smile, "And Frank has this inexplicable urge to protect you." He eyed her short and slender figure critically. "So we're going to help you. Now I've got to get back."

Sugar saw him to the door, seething. Then she picked up the map and went to the lab.

Japheth studied the map Sugar had spread out on the long stainless steel table. "What is your plan?" he asked. A Chessie sat attentively on each end of the table.

"We can't jump from here to the time we need. It's too close to their return. Also, they always went back so far that the house wasn't here, I think. So how do we get out without making unnecessary jumps? There's still so much we don't know. We might as well go see Uncle Max now." When they left, the two Chessies watched from the window.

\* \* \*

But at Maxwell Sweet's bungalow…

"I saw him just this morning," Sugar insisted. "Nurse Palmer said it was all right."

The nurse gave her what was intended to be a smile, though the rest of the world knew better. She was large, implacable, starched and white. Sugar thought fleetingly of the cliffs of Dover. "It's a good thing then that Nurse Palmer is no longer with us, Miss Sweet" she told Sugar. "Your uncle is too ill to see anyone. Mr. Walton tried to see him earlier too."

Sugar switched tactics. If Izzy couldn't charm his way in… "I'd appreciate it if you'd tell me how he's doing. He told me he was feeling better. Obviously he didn't want me to worry." She turned towards the kitchen. "I really do need something to drink." She glanced back at Japheth. "Wait here," she commanded. As the nurse stared at him with a cold, warning eye, Japheth dropped into a capacious wing chair and concentrated on the dark recesses of the fireplace.

In the kitchen, Sugar clasped a hot mug of coffee, leaned forward, and with all the humility she could muster, pleaded, "Please tell me about my uncle." She was still listening intently when the nurse suddenly heaved out of her chair and headed for the living room, leaving Sugar in her wake. She hove to in the empty living room.

"Oh dear," Sugar said desperately. "I forgot to tell him where the bathroom was.

"No problem," came Japheth's cheerful voice from behind them in the hall. "I found it." The nurse looked at him, suspicion written in capital letters in ice blue eyes.

"I do thank you, Nurse Warnock," Sugar said, backing down the long hall to the front door. Japheth had it open when she reached it. "I'll check back with you in a day or two." In the car, she locked the doors before starting up. "That was definitely a retreat," she said.

"Retreat nothing. That was a rout." Japheth looked back at the house with relief as they pulled away, but it wasn't till they had gone almost a block that he triumphantly pulled a notebook from inside his jacket. "Your uncle's been writing down everything he knows about operating the time machine for you; however, Samuels and Bartow were the experts."

* * *

Five days later, at 2:30 in the morning. Sugar stared upward as two sections of the roof slowly and silently separated.

Japheth stood beside her, holding the remote. "It works," he whispered and handed the device to Izzy. "I can control it from the time machine, too. This is just in case."

Izzy nodded. "You're all ready to go then. I'll cover for Frank and keep an eye on things at this end."

Frank stepped away from the machine where he and the Chessies had been standing. "We're almost all packed," he said softly.

Sugar's eyes widened and she fled to the kitchen. As the men loaded the two bodies, she concentrated intently on putting together something to munch on during the trip and tried not to think about what got munched on the last trip.

When the Chessies joined her in the kitchen, she was emptying ice into a thermos and talking to herself. As Rell kept watch in the doorway, Mingus spoke. "We want to go with you. We haven't been outside since we arrived; we grow restless. Perhaps we may be of service again," he added.

"They come," Rell warned.

"Of course," Sugar told them. She threw the sandwiches, chips, and soda in a bag, grabbed the thermos, and met the men at the door.

"No time to waste now," Izzy said.

Sugar nodded. She knew what he meant.

Inside the machine, Sugar sat between Japheth and Frank. Mingus and Rell climbed in behind the seat. Frank glanced at them, but said nothing.

"A safe and successful journey," Izzy said and stepped back.

"Don't forget to feed the cat," Japheth reminded him with a grin just before he slid the door closed. The grin faded when he looked at the control panel. "Let's do the check list, Sugar," he said.

"Power on," she told him. He hit the power switch, and a barely perceptible hum began.

"Hover," she said hoarsely, then cleared her throat and unclenched the hand that was beginning to crush the checklist.

The machine rose. Izzy retreated to the far wall. "Where's

the damn opening," Japheth said, trying to find it through the windows.

"Screen." Sugar pointed to a switch.

"What if it's a defense screen? We'd crush Izzy." Japheth began to sweat. His finger was poised over the Down button.

"Vision," Sugar and Frank said simultaneously. They both pointed. When Frank's hand brushed hers, Sugar was tempted to hang on to it or something—anything. She gritted her teeth. She kept her hand steady above the four buttons under Vision. "I'm hitting them all," she said, looking at the four blank screens over the controls.

Japheth didn't hesitate. "Do it," he said. The screens lit up as she pushed the buttons. There was one for each side of the machine. There was a collective hiss as the three humans drew in their breath. Rell was perched on the seat back almost on top of Sugar and breathing heavily in her ear. Mingus stared over Japheth's shoulder.

"We're rising," Frank pointed out.

"I've noticed," said Japheth between clenched teeth.

"There are two screens above the windows," Mingus said calmly in Sugar's mind. "I recognize them. They are camouflaged like those in the lab. Samuels and Bartow went to great lengths to hide things. But they would not make two such important controls inaccessible."

Sugar reached out and touched a finger on each side of the row of Vision control buttons. Nothing. She touched each side of the Monitor label, and the screens lit up.

The roof opening was still several feet above them and to their right. Japheth had already activated the retractable steering wheel. Tilting it gently, he guided the big machine slowly through the roof opening. Hovering above the house, Japheth closed the roof and ascended into the cloudy sky.

Sugar studied the panel compass and compared it with her own. They were being as careful as they could. She repeated the plan she'd written down and stuck in Uncle Max's notebook. "East to I-45 and then south to Galveston. If we have to, we'll land and check out the road signs. We do the time jump in the state park."

It wasn't difficult spotting the endless line of car lights

flowing north and south; and it wasn't long before they approached their goal. "We should see the island soon," Japheth told them after a quick glance at the odometer. "When I visited the park, I climbed as high as I could to see what it looked like from above. I hope I can find my parking place in the dark."

Japheth's hands were tight on the wheel as they drifted down to Galveston Island. He hovered above tree tops for long minutes studying the screens—set now for night vision—before setting the machine on the ground.

"Well done, Japheth," Sugar said. She peered out the tinted glass, but it was too dark to see anything, which was one reason they'd waited for this night. The other was Japheth's reconnaissance trip to Galveston.

"No point postponing it," Japheth said finally. "Let me look at the notebook one last time, though."

"Let's try to be a little more optimistic," she said, smiling briefly as she handed it over. Frank sat relaxed in his seat, watching the two Chessies as they sat on the seat back flanking Japheth and observing.

Referring constantly to the notebook, Japheth slowly made the dial settings. "Jump," he said at last. "How appropriate. I love their labels. I swear I'm going to make an operating manual though, but don't worry. I'll hide it in the *Tempus Fugit*. I know why they made everything so difficult."

"They certainly were careful, but it only took one mistake."

Sugar indicated the time setting. The two men looked at her.

"They were scientists," Frank said to reassure her.

"Well, no one's perfect," Japheth retorted. "Stand by for jump." He hit the button marked Jump. The numbers began to spin.

A single chime sounded when the numbers clicked to a stop. "It's just as dark," Sugar said uncertainly.

"Actually," Frank told her, "it's a little lighter. I've been on a lot of night stakeouts," he added.

"Good," Sugar said. "However, I'm just as glad we're going to the A&M campus here." She looked at her watch. "Time check. I've got 4:45. You pick us up tonight about 9:00 in the Gulf. You should be able to find us when we send up the flare."

Japheth nodded. "We'll wait back in the park till at least eight thirty. He glanced back at the cargo area. "Where's the food, Sugar?" he asked in sudden alarm. "I'm not going back there till I have to."

"Not to worry. It's right here," Rell told him.

"Of course," Sugar said. Frank didn't say anything, but it wasn't the first time he'd noticed apparent gaps in conversations.

It didn't seem as dark when Japheth dropped them off behind the campus building he'd also checked out on his trip down earlier in the week. Sugar stood close to Frank after the time machine lifted off. "You're used to prowling around in the dark, Francisco," she said. "You lead. I'll follow."

As soon as it got light they were on their way to rent the boat. Frank, wearing Bartow's faded brown coat and hat (washed out in the old cast iron bathtub with cold water, soap, and clenched teeth by Sugar), rented the fishing boat in Samuels' and Bartow's names. He picked up Sugar afterward.

By late afternoon they were well out in the Gulf, heading south and eating the lunch they'd bought before shoving off.

"It's rougher than I'd like," Sugar said uneasily as the boat pitched steadily southward.

"Yeah," Frank agreed. "He'll have to drop them on the deck." He looked at Sugar with concern. "You stay at the wheel and try to keep the boat steady."

By nine o'clock the storm had faded to the east, heading for Florida, and the sea was calmer. A few stars and a sliver of moon shone faintly through occasional clouds. "Now, I think," Frank said, readying the flare gun.

"No point waiting," she agreed. "We've plenty of flares if we need them."

Frank fired, and the sky lit up. As the flare slowly faded, they scanned the horizon. "We're a good ways out," Frank said, "but someone could have reported that flare by now. I was hoping we'd only need one."

"Wait a minute longer then," she urged as he contemplated the flares. Even as she finished speaking, a light blazed above their heads, and Japheth leaned out the open doorway of the time machine.

"I've got it on hover. How are we going to handle this?"

he yelled down to them.

"You hold it steady, Sugar, and watch for approaching boats." Frank left her at the wheel and moved to stand in the stern. "Shove 'em out, Japheth, and I'll try to keep them from going into the sea." He balanced lightly on the deck, bracing himself.

A yellowhaired form appeared in the doorway beside Japheth, and a Chessie launched itself to the deck. It landed beside Frank and skidded to the rail as the boat gave a sudden lurch. "Mingus is going to help you," Japheth shouted before he disappeared back into the *Tempus Fugit*.

"Coming down," he warned a couple minutes later, and he heaved the first body out. Rell caught him as he overbalanced and nearly followed it down. It landed heavily and rolled over once. Mingus and Frank wrestled it into the cabin. When they came back out, Rell was peering out of the doorway above. She drew back when she saw them, and moments later she and Japheth shoved the second body out. They'd aimed it for the cabin door this time, and it didn't take long to get it inside. Frank came out to retrieve the flares and returned to the cabin.

Sugar was still searching intently for other boats when Frank joined her at the wheel. She looked up into his face and murmured, "Thank you, Francisco."

He nodded. "Now we have ten minutes to get away from here." He led the way back. They stopped under the door of the time machine. He hoisted her up onto the top rail of the boat and held her until Japheth grabbed her wrists. Together he and Rell hauled her up.

Once she was clear, Frank leaped to the top rail, grabbed the door frame and pulled himself up. He was barely inside before Mingus was clawing his way in. "Hit it, man," Frank urged as he pushed and pulled at the tangle of bodies to give Japheth room.

Japheth took the machine straight up as Sugar found herself sitting on Frank's lap with Rell between them and Japheth. Mingus lay along the seat back, his head beside Japheth's.

They were several miles away and hovering when they saw the flash on the rear monitor. Frank considered for a moment. "Better go back and be sure it went down," he decided.

They circled the area for a half hour, looking for other boats as well as signs of wreckage before heading home. "Izzy should be starting his Galveston queries soon," Frank said.

Japheth looked at him with relief. "Thanks, Frank."

"I'll move if you want me to, Sugar," Rell told her. Sugar didn't bother to answer.

# Return to Neander

"MISSING PROFESSORS FOUND," Sugar read. "That's the headline anyway. It goes on to say Detectives Izaak Walton and Francisco Reyes traced the two men to Galveston where they'd rented a boat. There was an explosion reported out in the Gulf that night which could explain their disappearance. Professors S.A. Samuels and Adam Bartow of Texas A&M have been missing three weeks."

Japheth left his desk to look at the paper over her shoulder. "So that's what they looked like. I never saw them on campus; and what I saw of them here didn't look too good."

Sugar's fingers tightened on the paper. "Yes. I'm glad they're gone."

Japheth went on hurriedly, "There's a photo of Izzy and Frank, too. Frank looks the same as ever, but Izzy looks positively grim."

Sugar studied the picture thoughtfully. Frank was wearing his "off limits" look, but there was a tightness to Izzy's mouth that was unusual. Even his usually tousled red hair looked subdued. "He's not happy about covering up the truth, I think,"

Sugar said. "Understandable. He's a good cop."

"Could be it's harder on him because he wasn't there when we sunk the bodies in the Gulf," Japheth said, considering the photo. "I know one thing for sure though, Mr. and Mrs. Johnson wouldn't be happy to see their little boy's picture in the paper—not for blowing up evidence."

"Your parents live near here, don't they?" she asked, remembering that from the dossier Uncle Max had shown her.

"Yeah. That's one reason I went to A&M. What about yours?"

"Dead," she said briefly. She pushed back her long, cinnamoncolored hair. "Uncle Max raised me. That's why I majored in history—so I could help him in his work." She went back to studying the photo. Tall, though just a little taller than Izzy; dark, naturally; not polished and fragile like an elegant antique, but roughhewn and solid. Sugar put down the paper and started rummaging in her desk for a scissors.

Japheth grabbed the paper as it began to slide off Torquata who was sitting on the desk.

The big tabby swatted at it as it went by.

"Listen to this," Japheth said. He continued the story where Sugar had left off. "'They were working on some sort of secret project,' said Professor Norquist, a colleague. 'They never told me what it was, but Maxwell Sweet, the noted archeologist, was involved, I believe.' Professor Sweet, who has been ill, was unavailable for comment. Reporters and police were unable to get by Nurse Warnock, who is on guard duty at his house."

Sugar looked up, scissors in hand. "That reporter speaks from personal experience, I think." She smiled, remembering her own encounters with the nurse when visiting her uncle.

"Yeah." Japheth remembered his forbidden foray while Sugar distracted the nurse. That had been a close one, but he had escaped with the professor's notebook. Japheth handed the paper back and Sugar carefully cut out the photo of Izzy and Francisco.

"Aren't you going to cut out the whole article?" he asked.

"It might be suspicious if I collect articles on the disappearance, but a picture of my cousin..."

Japheth's gaze rested on Frank. "Of course," he said. Sugar put the newspaper photo in a drawer, closing it quickly as Torquata extended an exploratory paw. Japheth's gentle, long, brown fingers scratched him behind his ears.

As the gray tabby started purring, Japheth said, "Speaking of cats, where are the Chessies? I haven't seen them this morning."

"Still upstairs. I was surprised Rell wasn't waiting to see what I'd brought for breakfast, but when I yelled up the stairs, Mingus said they'd be down later."

Japheth looked puzzled. "It's been two days since we were out in the Gulf. Surely they're not still resting up from that."

She shrugged. "We still have one body left in the freezer. I'm going to ask Frank or Izzy to remove the bullet before we take him back. Unless you..."

"Hell no," he said, looking at her in alarm. "Ask Frank. It's his bullet."

"That bullet saved our lives," she reminded him. Her usually warm brown eyes were cold. "If I have to, I'll do it."

"Why not leave it in? What does it matter?" he asked. "My field is computer science," he reminded her defensively.

"You don't leave garbage strewn across the landscape, let alone the timescape," she said emphatically. "And we put things back where we found them." She sighed. "I just wish we knew for sure where they found him."

Japheth looked across the lab at the freezer that now held only one body. "There are coordinates and a map for Neander Valley on file. It's near Dusseldorf on the Rhine. We're going to have to assume that's where they went."

She nodded. "We'll leave him in the valley, definitely not in one of the caves. We'll have to cross the Atlantic in the past to avoid radar, guided missiles, and such."

"We make the time jump from here, then. I wish I knew how long that'll be. Too bad they didn't take any notes on that trip."

"Another trip?" asked Mingus. The big, catlike creature leaped onto the chair at the middle desk.

Sugar gave him a curious look. The coarse yellow hair of his coat appeared damp and smoother than usual. "I brought you breakfast," she said. "Egg McMuffins and hash browns. Where is Rell?"

"Still in bed. We were up late last night." He said it with an air of satisfaction. Japheth smiled.

"I'll call Izzy after breakfast," Sugar said, ignoring the two males, who appeared to be on a private wavelength.

* * *

Izzy arrived late that afternoon with a small satchel. "Borrowed it from the coroner's office," he informed Sugar.

"Japheth will help you if you need it. I'll be in the kitchen with Rell," she told them. "We're making up a list of supplies."

Izzy gave the satchel to Japheth. "You hold the tools. I'll perform the operation." He went to the freezer to remove the Neanderthal's body.

"Thanks, Izzy," Japheth said gratefully when the bullet had been removed. "Neat job," he added, looking at the head.

Izzy grunted and went to wash his hands. "Frank and I are busy finishing up the paperwork on the professors," he said when he came back. "You'll have to keep him on ice a while longer."

Japheth nodded, but said, after they put back the plastic-shrouded body, "She's impatient to get rid of him."

"Tough," Izzy told him and left, taking Frank's bullet with him.

"They're not in any hurry to leave or return the body, Sugar," Japheth told her after reporting on the operation.

"I noticed. Frank said they're working on a couple new cases, as a matter of fact. Izzy didn't mention that?"

"Nope. He didn't say much."

"Good," she told him. "We leave as soon as we're packed."

"Amazing how long he held on to that axe," Japheth said the next day as they put the cover on the box. They'd just finished packing the Neanderthal in dry ice for the trip.

"Biggest axe I ever saw," Sugar said, "especially when he was waving it at me. I would have kept it for a souvenir except we probably should return it too."

"He sure did a number on that cage door with it," Japheth said, glancing at the cages lined up against the wall in the time machine room. The one at the far end was battered and bent. "I've been reading up on Neanderthals," he continued. "They didn't have axes like that."

"Really," she said skeptically. "So where did it come from?"

"I would have said from inside the time machine, except he obviously used it to break out of his cage."

Sugar considered the axe thoughtfully. "So, should we keep it after all?"

"I wouldn't want to screw up history by introducing the axe. And what if he's not from there or then?"

"We take it with us and decide there. We'll study the locals," she said with enthusiasm. They were interrupted by Rell's arrival.

"Ready for another time trip, Rell?" Japheth grinned at the Chessie who'd just arrived. She looked at him with yellow, slitted, almost invisible eyes for a moment.

"Traveling is fun." The thought was emphatic and eager. She widened her eyes and grinned. Torquata was sniffing interestedly around the cages. He usually accompanied the humans now when they went into the lab or the room where *Tempus Fugit* was; but he still gave the Chessies a wide berth.

Mingus appeared, carrying food packages. He walked on his hind legs now. They were still getting used to his bipedal stance. His hips adjusted for it, he'd told them.

"Tools and all the supplies I can think of." Japheth shoved the last box inside the cargo area and closed the rear doors. "I just wish I knew how long the trip will take."

"You've been figuring for two days now, using their data from the other trips. And we packed more than enough fuel and food," Sugar said reassuringly. "The only thing that worries me is carrying the extra fuel in the cargo area."

"The Zircaloy cladding material I found in the basement vault should do the trick. But like the fuel, Samuels didn't leave a clue as to where he got it."

"Uncle Max has no idea. He's pretty sure Bartow didn't know either. Those two were damn careful…" she looked at Japheth, "…except on their last trip."

"Remember what Frank said. They were scientists, after all." He sighed. "He meant, of course, that he and Izzy would take care of us. I hate to admit it, but I'd feel safer if they were going along."

"They're busy, and I'm tired of bodies in my freezer. We have the Chessies; we go now." She grabbed the notebook Japheth had gotten from Uncle Max and pulled out the checklist.

Japheth nodded. Actually, he decided, he was glad to be on his own. Frank and Izzy treated him and Sugar like children. At least once he'd felt more like a kindergarten infant than a college graduate with an important, though very secret, job.

"All aboard," he called out, and the two Chessies scrambled in. Rell staked out the end of the bench seat, next to Sugar, while Mingus settled for the top of a big box that covered the fuel access door in the floor. Japheth climbed in last and slid the door shut. Mingus peered over his shoulder at the control panel.

"Power on," Sugar said, finger at the top of the list. Japheth hit the power switch; the unobtrusive hum began, and he activated the roof mechanism. One section of the roof slowly separated above them, revealing the night sky. Rising slowly, they hovered for a moment overhead to make sure the roof closed, before going up higher preparatory to making the time jump.

As usual, it was only a gray blur once they were wherever they went when making the jump. The monitors over the control panel and the wraparound windows showed only what appeared to be empty space. Sugar watched the hypnotic march of numbers while Japheth kept a watchful eye on the panel. At last Rell nudged Sugar emphatically.

"Let's do lunch," she said, with a flash of teeth and humor. She climbed onto the seat back, then dropped behind it and slid open the cargo door.

"I'm not really hungry, Rell," Sugar told her, staring uneasily at the open door.

"Later," Japheth seconded her, concentrating with passionate intent on the controls. "I wish I could see where we were," he muttered.

Eventually Sugar overcame her reluctance and joined Rell and Mingus. "Picnics are fun," Rell said, before making her final decision between a cookie and a Twinkie for dessert.

Sugar sneered at the Twinkie. "Goopy goopies," she said and grabbed the cookie. Japheth rarely left the controls, usually eating and sleeping on the bench seat. They'd rigged a screen around the chemical toilet and brought along a large supply of HandiWipes since water would be in short supply.

* * *

It was the morning of the third day when the numbers clicked slowly to a stop. "The last interglacial period, according to their records," Sugar murmured.

"Good. I wouldn't want to travel all that way over ice." Japheth spread out his maps, along with papers full of figures, compass directions, and latitude and longitude notations.

Sugar picked up the map on top of the pile and read the note attached. "Northeast for a little over 8,000 miles." Japheth snorted. "I know that's rough," she told him, "but we do the fine tuning after that." She patted the pile. "It's a good thing the Rhine has that nifty little hook by Dusseldorf."

"That was now; this is then," he said. "Besides, the Rhine is full of hooks."

"Well, the Dussel runs into the Rhine, and we'll just pick a likely looking valley. It probably doesn't matter that much. He'll be just as dead no matter where we dump him."

They came out of the time field just before dawn, and watched with appreciation as the sun rose over a land with no signs of civilization. The trip was a lot more interesting with scenery, and they spent two nights camping out. The Chessies reverted to traveling on all fours. They could cover more territory that way.

"75,000 years ago," said Sugar, marveling as she walked around *Tempus Fugit* in a big circle at their first stop. They'd picked the biggest clearing they could find. "I wish I could be sure what was around here then. I'd really like to explore a little. But I can't run as fast as the Chessies if something should start chasing me." She glanced enviously at Mingus and Rell who stood on a nearby hill staring off into the distance.

Japheth shivered a little and pulled his jacket tighter. "Is the ice age coming or going?" he demanded. He considered the terrain cautiously. "It's open enough, and they can warn us if something takes an interest in us. We can take a couple guns—just to scare animals off with; I know we have to avoid killing them," he added quickly.

"I'd feel better with a gun," Sugar admitted. She was relieved to see that Japheth was as eager to explore as she was. They looked around until dark. "Modern plants, grass, and deciduous trees—that's for sure; I bet it's more interesting farther back," mused Sugar, a little disappointed.

Japheth paused at the door he'd just opened. "It seems tame all right, but anything without dinosaurs is fine with me."

Sugar gazed at him, unable to restrain a giggle. "Ah, you're one of those kids who saw *Jurassic Park* at too tender an age."

"Mom kept her hands over my eyes during most of the movie as I recall, but I didn't try to peek out much," he admitted. "What about you?"

"I saw it on tape later with Uncle Max. We critiqued it for scientific errors. And I still say feeding tree branches to giant herbivores is not real bright."

Mingus leaped gracefully through the open door and moved down the seat, making room for Rell and the other two to enter. "There are no such creatures here though, right?" he asked.

"No, but we sleep with the doors shut and someone on watch," Japheth said. "I'll take the first watch." Sugar went on into the cargo area and lowered the hammocks; it was more comfortable than she expected. She'd always preferred a firm mattress.

She slept soundly until Japheth woke her. "It's early yet," he whispered, "but there's the first sign of life sniffing around. I thought you might like to see them."

Sugar spilled out of her hammock, dropping in front of the window. She stared out in thrilled amazement. "Wow for sure," she said. "A sabertoothed tiger. I never thought to be so lucky."

"There's another one around," Japheth whispered. As he spoke, the second tiger, even more massive than the first, joined its mate and reared up against the time machine, bracing itself with its front paws as it sniffed curiously. They were face to face, though the big cats couldn't see inside the tinted windows. The nails scraped loudly down the desert-camouflage-painted side of the converted van as it dropped to the ground.

"Easy on the paint job, kitties." Sugar spoke softly, as Mingus and Rell stood on each side of her, quietly observing.

"Look at those teeth," Rell muttered uneasily. "If I'd known there were creatures like them around, I'd never have gotten out."

"About ten inches, I'd say," Japheth told her. They watched until the tigers trotted off into the night and their short tails disappeared into the brush.

It was past time for Sugar's watch to begin, but she had to force Japheth to go to bed. "No telling what tomorrow will bring," she told him finally.

She was grateful it was her watch because it took her a couple hours to unwind—both from the excitement and the re-alization of the dangers they were bound to face. *But I'm enjoying it*, she acknowledged to herself. *I probably should cultivate a more scholarly attitude; I didn't even think of measuring them.*

\* \* \*

The next morning she found Japheth kneeling by the pug marks. "I didn't bring anything to measure these with," he said, annoyed at himself. "I was only thinking of surviving the trip, but I'd say they're close to a foot long."

Sugar got her purse out of *Tempus Fugit* and pulled out a windup tape and small notebook. "I always carry these," she said, "but we're going to have to make up some sort of study kit." She measured the tracks. "You were right—not quite a foot," she said, "and they're almost as wide."

"That's the big one. We'll need plaster for making casts too," he added.

He shaded his eyes, facing east. "We're almost to the ocean."

"Yes, I know," she said, puzzled. "I wanted to spend the night inland. Do you have a sudden yen to go to the beach?"

He turned back to her. "I didn't pack an inflatable raft."

"We've used the hover mode over water before—in the Gulf. Ah, are you worrying about crashing?"

"You know I like to be prepared. Now I'm wondering if I've forgotten anything else—something that could be really important."

She laughed. "You do like to worry, which, strangely enough, makes me feel more secure. But I believe the *Tempus Fugit* is seaworthy. We've studied the specs after all, and we could make paddles or sails if we had to."

He looked at her, drew a deep breath, and ran a hand through his short, tightlycurled hair. "We do make a good crew, I think." He glanced at the Chessies, who were sitting on top of the time machine, keeping watch. "Let's set sail, me hearties." A short time later, having taken advantage of the great outdoors, they left.

The flight over the ocean, empty except for an occasional glimpse of its inhabitants, was uneventful; Japheth took a quick inventory before they ventured forth, however, to have everything ready that might be needed for sails, oars, or a raft. The butterfly-blue expanse of water was beautiful, but they were glad to leave it behind. They'd angled northeast to what would be Europe. Now, as they passed over thickly wooded terrain, Japheth and Sugar constantly searched through their accumulation of maps to make what comparisons they could.

Finally they stopped. "Two rivers and a valley. It's deeper in the future, but I don't know how long that took." Japheth scanned the valley they'd set down in with a frown.

"Could be caves up there, but it probably wouldn't be wise to explore them," Sugar said regretfully. Rell stayed close, but Mingus had already made a wide circle and was spiraling out.

"You two keep watch while Japheth and I get out the box," Sugar told Rell. They pushed it out through the back doors and removed the cover.

"Just in time," Japheth said through clenched teeth. "Let's just turn it over." They did, letting the body and the remaining dry ice spill over the ground. Then they quickly put the cover back on and slid the box back inside the machine.

"We have company." Mingus' warning message touched them both, and Japheth reached out to slam shut the back doors.

"Wait," Sugar told him.

"Some of us may need to get in that way. How many, Mingus, and have they seen you?"

"They haven't seen us yet. There are only three of them, and I'm behind them. Rell is behind *Tempus Fugit;* I've told her to stay there. What should we do?"

"They've undoubtedly seen the body; they haven't seen us kill him. We'll have a funeral service. They should understand that. That'll give us time to make a plan."

Japheth had knelt down before she finished speaking. He quickly straightened the body and laid the big axe beside it. He moved to stand at the head and told Sugar, "You stand at his feet. That's probably more in keeping with their culture."

"So was cannibalism," she retorted "Can you see them?"

"Yes. They're behind you. They're curious and respectful, I think. Not an axe in sight, by the way. They all have spears. Those pathetic little lashings loosen in the dew, the mist and the rain, you know. You have to tighten them every time they get wet."

"Where'd you learn that?" she asked, trying to look humble and unaware. Once the cave men knew they'd been spotted, they'd have to move fast.

"Kipling—he wrote some great adventure stories. I remember reading about Devil-in-the-Dusk—that was a wolf—and sea serpents, Kim and Mowgli, and how long should this service go on? I'm afraid to stop talking."

"I suppose it could go on for a long time, but I draw the line at singing and dancing. Know any appropriate gestures?

We can finish up by throwing dust in the air, but what do we do after that?"

"Finish soon," advised Mingus. "The biggest one, who is also the leader, has decided to take that axe. He's never seen one like it and is thinking about going for it—NOW!"

Sugar leaped forward and grabbed the axe. "Start the machine now, Japheth," she yelled. "If you take the axe, they'll be after you. Come on, Rell. We're getting in the back. Mingus, can you give them a few swipes as you come through them?"

The big Neanderthal was heading for Sugar at a dead run. It took the other two a few seconds to start after him. Like alligators, she thought, they look so slow until they start moving. She threw the axe into the time machine and jumped in, shutting one door and looking for Mingus and Rell.

The biggest of the three was still a few feet ahead of his companions and almost to the open door. He was wearing only a skimpy, hairy loincloth and a triumphant snaggletoothed grin.

Sugar had one hand on the door; she felt the vibration that meant Japheth was ready to go. In her other hand she held a rifle ready to use as a club. She was bringing it forward to ram the lead attacker in the stomach, when she heard a rising, high-pitched shriek. She looked up to see Mingus coming through the other two Neanderthals. Sugar caught just a glimpse as he sent the short and thickbodied men sprawling.

The Neanderthal confronting Sugar flinched and hesitated, and Rell bowled him over and leapt into the machine. He dropped his spear when he fell; he was reaching for it when Sugar leaned out of the machine and grabbed it as Mingus cleared her back. Broad, squarelooking hands clutched futilely as Sugar threw herself in, pulled the door shut, and yelled, "Tell Japheth to split."

An enraged face that was all eyes and nose and no chin and more muzzle than mouth was glaring in the back window when they took off. Sugar hurried up front and crawled over the seat back, being careful not to stab Japheth with the spear. "I got his spear," she said, feeling suddenly guilty.

Japheth nodded. "Good. We'll add it to our collection. I was thinking we should have a museum. We have to do something with all the stuff we'll be collecting." He looked up at the monitors above the control panel. "Where to now? You don't want to go back yet, do you?"

Sugar glanced sideways at him and grinned. "I would like to look around a little more while we're here. I was afraid you'd want to go home after that. Where are we?"

"The other end of the valley. See over there to your right—a stream. Let's land and check it out. Take samples and compare it with our water. That'd be an interesting experiment."

Japheth set the *Tempus Fugit* down gently a few feet away from the bank of the rushing stream, and they scrambled out quickly. After Mingus did his exploratory spiral, Rell persuaded them to have a picnic by the water. "This is fun," Sugar said, after finishing her sandwich. "By the way, Mingus, that was you howling, wasn't it?" She studied the Chessie curiously. She'd never heard them vocalize before that.

"I thought that'd distract them," Mingus told her. "They've got quick reflexes though. After I knocked the first one down, the second clipped some hair from my neck with a sharp stone he was carrying before he went down."

"Hand axe," said Japheth, looking up with sudden interest. "I'd sure like one of those for our collection."

"Maybe next time," Sugar said. "We don't want to get greedy or careless. And I don't think I'll ever try bringing one back for tests."

"Returning them'd take another trip and waste fuel," Japheth added thoughtfully. "This," he said, indicating their surroundings, "is probably safer than getting more fuel would be, even if we knew where they obtained it."

"True," Sugar agreed as she stood up. "Let's explore a little longer, but we'd better not go far."

"I think I'll put on another sweater under my jacket," Japheth said. "It's getting colder. Wait for me."

"You're right." Sugar looked towards the west. "The sun will be going down more quickly because we're in a valley. We'd better decide where to spend the night. If those hunters we met earlier are determined enough, they might just follow in the direction we took."

"Which way?" Japheth asked when he returned. Sugar looked at the Chessies with sudden speculation. "Mingus, can you read people without seeing them or knowing their location?"

"There's a hunter coming downstream toward us with news of a big animal asleep in a cave, and there is a group of people further downstream from us."

"Yes!" said Japheth, with appropriate gestures. "A hibernating cave bear—the theories are correct. And that explains those patches of snow in the shade. It's still winter, unless it's almost winter."

"Probably," agreed Sugar. "It's not quite cold enough for an ice age. Let's check out the people and see what they're up to. What about *Tempus Fugit*?"

"The hunter is in a hurry," Mingus informed them. "Even if he notices it, I don't think he's going to stop."

"We'd better hurry if we're going to beat him to those people," Rell added. "That's where he's headed." They hugged the bank as they headed downstream. It took almost an hour to reach their quarry. Two women knelt scraping an enormous skin, while a man sat nearby, patiently chipping stones. A young boy sat next to him, concentrating for some minutes before attempting to imitate him—again, they deduced from the flakes surrounding him. A much younger child played with a wooden toy close to the women.

They lay prone and watched from upwind in a spot Mingus guided them to. "It's a good thing the water is so noisy or they would undoubtedly hear us crashing about," he said.

Though it got colder and darker as they lay on the ground, Sugar was reluctant to give the word to go back, so that they were still there when the hunter finally arrived. He conveyed his news with guttural sounds and pantomime, and the whole group gathered together and returned with the hunter upstream.

"All of them went!" Sugar exclaimed softly when they'd been gone about fifteen minutes.

"So should we," Japheth said uneasily. "It's almost dark. I'm surprised they're wandering around at night."

"They're heading home," Mingus explained. "They'll tackle the cave bear in the morning. They need everyone to help carry after they kill and butcher it."

"No one has spotted *Tempus Fugit*," Rell said. "Let's go before anyone or anything does."

"In a minute," Japheth said, kneeling where the man and boy had been working. "Look at all these great flakes—flint, I think; they'd have taken them if they wanted them. I wouldn't think it could possibly affect the future to take a few back."

"Help yourself," Sugar said as she joined him. "I've got a spear after all. I'm sure he can make another one easily enough. They must lose them all the time."

There was a flash of amusement from Mingus. "Actually he's planning to make an axe. I picked him up on my last scan. He and his friends have denned up for the night. I think, from the wariness in their thoughts, we should be getting back."

Japheth hurriedly filled his jacket pockets with flakes. It was almost full dark when they reached the *Tempus Fugit* and definitely colder. However, keeping warm was no problem; they were moving as quickly as they could to keep ahead of the creature Mingus told them had picked up their trail.

"What was it?" Sugar asked breathlessly once they were safely inside with the doors locked.

"I don't know, but it's definitely hungry," Mingus told her. His small ears were down and his eyes invisible in what was obviously a defensive reaction.

Sugar activated the monitors, switching over to night vision. "It's staying in the trees, so that I can't get a good look at it," she said. "Ah, look there," she exclaimed, pointing, "did you see that head?"

"Yes. Rather bearlike, but not as big—sort of like a cross between a bear and a wolf. I don't know what it could be. What do you think, Mingus?" Japheth asked, eyes glued to the monitor.

"It's sort of disappointed and annoyed. It doesn't think it can dig us out of our cave." Mingus' thought held definite relief.

"I'll take the first watch," Sugar said. "The rest of you get some sleep. We should probably leave about sunup before any of the Neanderthals are up and about."

"You don't want to take in the cavebear hunt?" Japheth asked, raising his eyebrows in mock surprise.

"Of course I do," she said coolly, "but I don't think it's feasible. You'll have to develop some kind of remote camera when we get back. It'll have to utilize some sort of robotics," she went on thoughtfully. "Do you know anything about robots?"

she asked the Chessies suddenly.

"No," Mingus said briefly, and his thought was dark and grim. Sugar wondered again about their origins. She was pretty sure some day they'd confide in her. She was certain also that they were trapped here.

"We'll go home in the morning," was all she said.

"Home," echoed Rell. Her thought was as sunny as Mingus' had been bleak.

# Flashback

Sugar pushed her chair back so that she could see past Rell who was sitting in the chair at the middle desk and amusing herself by slowly spinning around on it. "I've been thinking, Japheth," she said, "about where to go next." She shuddered a little, thinking of their first two trips. "This time I want to do something fun," she added.

"That's for sure," he agreed, looking back at her from where he sat at his computer. He ran his hand through his closecropped and tightly curled hair, then studied his long, brown fingers thoughtfully. "At least I've stopped twitching. What did you have in mind?"

Sugar's gaze rested briefly on Mingus sprawled on the floor close by Rell's chair. "I thought we might start off by backtracking Samuels and Bartow. With all that data in their records, it would be easier to get experience that way. Why not, for instance, go back to where they found Mingus and Rell."

Rell stopped spinning to face Sugar. Then slowly her eyes disappeared into the coarse yellow hair. Mingus sat up and scratched one ear. This was one of the times when they looked not only incredibly catlike, but reminded Sugar of the Cheshire cat they'd been named for.

Rell's eyes suddenly reappeared. "Are you planning to leave us there?" she asked suspiciously.

"Of course not, Rell," Sugar said indignantly and aloud. Though it was rare that she didn't communicate verbally with the two telepaths, she had attempted it on occasion.

"I've got it," Japheth said as he studied the computer screen. "That's a heck of a long time ago—during the Quaternary ice age. Do you have any idea of how many millions of years that is?!"

"Only about two," she said impatiently. "To catch dinosaurs, we have to go back a hell of a lot farther. And Samuels and Bartow did it. What's important is how much fuel we'll need."

"Coming right up, Miss Sweet," he responded formally.

She sighed. "Let's not get excited. We can do it. That is,

I can do it with your help. That's why I asked you to join the project, Japheth," she reminded him.

Japheth nodded absently as he studied the fuel formula he'd pulled from his desk drawer. "It doesn't take as much fuel to go back as it does to get started and slow down, or go halfway around the world. This is straight back in time, and this trip we'll have their notes. They weren't able to write them up their last trip," he added soberly.

Sugar shivered. "We won't have to guess how long it'll take either."

"If you two are through," Mingus interrupted, "I have a suggestion. How about going back a year and three months earlier than that?"

Rell recoiled, laying her small ears back and practically hissing. "They're not stupid," Mingus told Rell, "and I am curious. I'd like to see it happen."

Rell spat something directed only at Mingus, but Sugar was sure she caught the word "fool".

"He's right, Rell," she ventured. "We're not stupid. It's pretty obvious you're not from earth. Even though you seem designed for the cold weather back then."

"Actually we were adapted for the desert," Mingus said.

"That was my next guess," Sugar said coolly. "But really, Rell, don't worry about it. Honestly, we're just curious." She looked hopefully at Japheth.

"That's right, Rell, we're your friends. You're safe here," Japheth told her earnestly, "or there or then. Whatever."

"And warm and well fed. And don't forget tacos," Sugar added.

Rell's coarse, yellow coat smoothed out and her ears came up. If she'd had a tail, it would have stopped lashing. "So let's get started," Sugar said decisively. Japheth looked at her and sighed loudly.

\* \* \*

Almost a week later, they stood next to *Tempus Fugit* surrounded by piles of boxes. Sugar considered the vanlike time machine with its wraparound windows. "That camouflage paint job isn't going to blend in at all," she worried.

Japheth shrugged, not looking up. He was loading the fuel

into the floor behind the front seat. Handling it always made
him nervous. When he'd finished, he looked up. "That should
give us plenty of power," he said, sounding relieved.

"There'll be no one there to see, Sugar," Mingus reassured
her.

"Good. Now let's find out if we can stuff all these supplies
inside," she said and grabbed a box and slid it in. Japheth checked
the label and shoved it out of sight.

"We have all the time in the world, Sugar," he said sharply
as she slid another box in. "I have to check these labels before
I stow them."

"I know, I know," she said, stifling her eagerness. "You
want to be prepared in case anything goes wrong. If it does
though, our food won't last nearly long enough." She shivered
as she contemplated a cold future in the past.

"That's why I have practically a whole workshop packed,
too." He sounded confident, and Sugar relaxed. If he wasn't
worried, everything should be okay.

When everything was packed and fastened down and
the door to the cargo section secured, Sugar stashed their cold
weather gear behind the seat. Rell and Mingus settled down on
top of it.

"Now for the check list, Sugar." Japheth studied dials
and punched buttons as she read it off. When he hit the power
switch, they listened for the barely perceptible hum; then he set
the temporal destination. The numbers began to roll by, faster
and faster backward.

Time went by slowly inside the time machine. At last
Japheth stretched, loosening muscles cramped from his intense
concentration. "I'm glad we can utilize their data. I'd go crazy
wondering how long it would take to go back each trip. According to Samuels and Bartow, it'll be just 32 hours. You might as
well go back and check out the living quarters now."

Sugar nodded, though it took an effort to drag her eyes
away from the procession of years unwinding on the dial. There
was nothing to be seen through the windows. They were going
too fast.

She crawled over the back of the bench seat, slid the cargo
door open and fell in, making her way down the narrow aisle

that ran between stacks of boxes held in place by bungee cords. The cubicle that contained the chemical toilet was all the way at the back. There would be no bathing en route.

There was no need for heat while they were travelling, but they had a heater if they needed it when they arrived. Japheth's was the first shift; Sugar had to pull rank to send him to his hammock when it was her turn. Mingus pushed him bodily through the door when he would have turned back to remind Sugar to wake him if anything went wrong. He arrived early for his next shift.

Sugar yawned and looked across at Rell who was swaying gently. She scrambled out of her own hammock and went up front. "Anybody hungry?" she asked, smothering another yawn.

Japheth looked up from monitoring Mingus at the control panel. "Sounds good. I'd like eggs and bacon and a side order of hash browns."

"Me too. Too bad we have to settle for cheese sandwiches." Sugar had decided that cutting down on cooking and dish washing would save on water. Next trip she'd do some experimenting though. Now she looked at the windows. "I wish we could see what's happening out there. Isn't there some way we could rig a video camera?"

"Samuels tried," Japheth said thoughtfully, "but he never succeeded. I may have an idea about that, however. I should at least be able to get something when we start slowing down. I would probably have to hook it up to the chronometer; the amount of tape we'd need would be prodigious."

"Sounds like fun," Sugar said, smiling at his enthusiasm. "Enjoy yourself."

Japheth looked at her seriously. "I wouldn't have had this opportunity without you, Sugar. I appreciate it."

She was pleased, but had to say honestly, "I'm lucky to have you. Don't ever think I don't appreciate that."

They settled into a routine, but when Japheth said, "We should be coming up on it soon," they crowded in front so that they all heard the warning ping. Japheth concentrated on the controls, mouth tense, in case a manual override was needed.

The numbers kept slowing, however, until they stopped. They stared out the tinted windows for several minutes even though there wasn't much to see. Then Sugar leaned over the back of the seat to grab their winter clothes. She and Japheth immersed themselves in layers of clothes until they could hardly move. She shoved her long, cinnamonbrown hair back, covering a face paler than usual almost completely.

"This would make a great advertisement for L.L. Bean," she said lightly, pausing at the door. Then Japheth slid it open, and they stepped out into a planetary winter. Everything everywhere was white. Drifting snow whispered around their feet and occasionally moaned and billowed in the frequent gusts of wind.

They stood on a slight rise with the time machine behind them. Snow spread out in a level carpet of white, unmarked as far as the eye could see. "It's beautiful," said Sugar. Her breath quivered in a cloud of frosty white. It was so cold, she listened for it to thud to the ground.

"Thank God the ice didn't come this far south," said Japheth fervently.

Mingus moved out slowly and stopped several feet away. "That direction," he said, facing northeast. Rell paced deliberately over to join him. "It won't be long now, according to my calculations," he continued. "The machine calibrations are fine enough … Look there." He pointed a paw.

A dark streak arced through the dotted Swiss sky, skipped twice, and pancaked to the earth, melting snow spreading out in a syrupy flow after it landed. Almost immediately there was a flash, brilliant but soundless.

"Radiation," yelled Japheth. He pushed Sugar ahead of him towards the time machine.

"No radiation," said Mingus, "just dissipating energy."

Japheth looked at him incredulously. "Even so, don't you think we were a little close?"

"Well, my calculations were slightly off," Mingus admitted. They gazed at the ship in silence while snowflakes sizzled as they touched down upon it; a circular bare patch surrounded it as the snow melted.

"What happened next?" Sugar asked, shivering from excitement and cold.

"We were immobilized for a time while the ship cooled. Then we probed the countryside."

"We'll have to leave soon before we're spotted," Rell said sharply.

"We saw no signs of life anywhere," Mingus continued. "We decided to hibernate—there were facilities for that—and set the proximity alarm. Fortunately, it was only a year and three months later—your time—before Samuels and Bartow arrived."

"Why fortunately?" Sugar asked.

"The ship's systems were more badly damaged than we realized. By then we were a big, snowcovered hill. We ran out and frolicked around the time machine. We didn't realize what it was then. We were so ingratiating that they took us along back. They never had a clue."

"They did, of course," Sugar told him. "Sensors took readings of your ship. That's why they stopped; an alarm went off. They never connected it with you two though; and they didn't analyze the recording until they got back. A return trip was on the agenda."

"We should go, I think," Rell urged again, "to avoid confusing ourselves on the ship or meeting ourselves outside."

"She's right," seconded Japheth, thinking about time travel paradoxes he had been reading up on. "And it's cold out here for us desert and tropical types." Sugar agreed reluctantly and turned back to the *Tempus Fugit*. Inside, it took two to shove the door shut. The cold was affecting the mechanism.

"Good thing we didn't wait any longer." Japheth reset the controls. The numbers started moving forward.

Sugar looked at the Chessies. "Thanks, Mingus, for letting us see that and for trusting us."

"Yeah," said Japheth. "I suppose, though, that back where you came from, everyone—humanoids and nonhumanoids—get along fine. No prejudice or shit like that."

Mingus and Rell looked at him. Sugar and Japheth felt their amusement. "Actually," Rell said, "we were escaping. That's why we crashed. We weren't familiar with the controls."

# About the Author

Joy V. Smith was born on a Wisconsin farm and went to the University of Wisconsin – Oshkosh; and she was first published in college, but she's been writing and making little books—with covers!—since she was a kid. She writes mostly science fiction, her favorite genre. Her stories have been published in print magazines, ezines, and anthologies; and her SF has been published in two audiobooks, including *Sugar Time*.

She also has two collections of SF and fantasy reprints: *The Doorway and Other Stories* and *Aliens, Animals, and Adventure;* her SF ebooks include *Hidebound, Pretty Pink Planet* and *Hot Yellow Planet* (the sequel). She lives in Florida with Blizzard the Snow Princess and Bryn the Flying Corgi.

www.ingramcontent.com/pod-product-compliance
Lightning Source LLC
Chambersburg PA
CBHW022054170626
46808CB00003B/1465

## Praise for *Alice on the Shelf*

"*Alice on the Shelf* is a wonderfully entertaining and interesting take on Lewis Carroll's classic. I read it in one sitting, always wanting to know what was coming next. Bill Gauthier is a great new writer, and I can't wait to see what he comes up with next."
– John R. Little, author of the Stoker-winning novella *Miranda*, *The Gray Zone*, and *The Memory Tree*

"...a very clever and sometimes humorous fantasy with children's beloved characters; however, this is definitely not a story for young children...I enjoyed it very much, and I highly recommend it."
– Sheri White, *Horrorgy*

"I liked this one quite a lot. The story unfolds neatly and the allusions give it an extra dimension."
– Don D'Ammassa

"One of Gauthier's strengths seems to be to...tap into his own experiences and turn that into a good story...the mark of a good writer is one that can crystallize this into good fiction."
– Trevor Nordgen, *Dark Discoveries*

"Bill Gauthier has taken the beloved stories of our childhood and created a new incarnation for them in *Alice on the Shelf*. The characters are well-developed, even the more familiar ones, and Gauthier's prose calls up some very vivid imagery. The pacing is good throughout which makes for an engaging story. I read *Alice* in one sitting. The end contains a great twist that I never saw coming. *Alice* is a definite "get" for your book collection."
– Colleen Wanglund, *The Horror Fiction Review*

"The parody of *Alice* is an effective foil for Gauthier's sardonic humor, and provides ready-made characters to manipulate in truly bizarre ways. However, the story is not overly dependent on Lewis Carroll's work; instead, *Alice on the Shelf* functions as a tribute, and a ghastly interpretation of the original. Recommended.

– Sheila Shedd, *Monster Librarian*

"Gauthier weaves a macabre tale of not only Alice's world, but Dorothy's world, and other assorted fairy tales as well as references to some modern horror classics. He does an absolutely wonderful job of combining all these into a fast paced visceral joy ride into the strange and wonderful."

– Peter Schwotzer, *Famous Monsters of Filmland*